Clare's Goodbye

*To Michael
and Jenny,
Benedict,
Jacob and
Clare—LG*

*For Claudio,
caro fratello
mio, con amore
—AP*

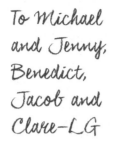

Little Hare Books
an imprint of
Hardie Grant Egmont
Ground Floor, Building 1, 658 Church Street
Richmond, Victoria 3121, Australia

www.littleharebooks.com

First published 2017
Reprinted 2017

Cataloguing-in-Publication details are available
from the National Library of Australia

978 1 760127 52 7 (hbk.)

This book was edited by Margrete Lamond and Alyson O'Brien
Production management by Sally Davis
Designed by Hannah Janzen
Produced by Pica Digital, Singapore
Printed through Asia Pacific Offset
Printed in Shenzhen, Guangdong Province, China

6 5 4 3 2

The illustrations in this book were created with charcoal,
pencil, coloured pencil, collage and watercolour.

Clare's Goodbye

Libby Gleeson  Anna Pignataro

LITTLE HARE
www.littleharebooks.com

Rosie and Jacob sat under
the lemon tree.

'Come on, Clare,' said Rosie, 'it's time to say goodbye. Goodbye to everything.'

Clare didn't move from the back step.

Jacob grabbed Rosie's hand. 'We have to say goodbye to the tree house.'

They walked in a circle around the tree.
Jacob climbed the first two steps of the ladder
and rested his face on the bark.

'Come and say goodbye
to your snails' nest, Clare,' Rosie called.

Clare shook her head.

Rosie pushed the box with her foot.
Empty snail shells
and dead grass fell out.

'And the place where
we buried Blossom,' said Jacob.

He picked some dandelions and sprinkled them over the mound of dirt. 'We should dig her up and take her with us.'

'Don't be stupid,' said Rosie.

They went down the path to the sandpit. All the toys had gone.

'We could write "goodbye" here.'
Rosie dug her fingers into the sand.

Jacob tried to follow the letters Rosie had made.

Still Clare said nothing.

They hid behind the water tank and watched the men take the lounge chairs down the driveway.

Then they took the television and the boxes of books.

Dad and Uncle John took the kitchen table and the chairs.

Mum collected all the pot plants.

'Where's Clare?' said Jacob.

They looked around the yard.

Then the kitchen.

The empty lounge room.

The dining room.

The front verandah.

The house felt
cold and empty.

A noise came from
their old bedroom.
Jacob pushed the
door open.

In the room there was only Clare
and she was dancing.

Her eyes were
closed, her arms
spread wide.

Around and
around she went.

Rosie and Jacob
watched for
a moment.

Then Jacob stepped into the
room and Rosie followed.

They spread their arms
and silently joined the
dance,
dancing goodbye ...

to their house.